STAR WARS®

THE CLONE WARS™

A Jedi Adventure in 3-D

By Pablo Hidalgo

Grosset & Dunlap
An Imprint of Penguin Group (USA) Inc.
LucasBooks

GROSSET & DUNLAP
Published by the Penguin Group
Penguin Group (USA) Inc., 375 Hudson Street, New York, New York 10014, USA
Penguin Group (Canada), 90 Eglinton Avenue East, Suite 700,
Toronto, Ontario M4P 2Y3, Canada (a division of Pearson Penguin Canada Inc.)
Penguin Books Ltd., 80 Strand, London WC2R 0RL, England
Penguin Group Ireland, 25 St. Stephen's Green, Dublin 2, Ireland (a division of Penguin Books Ltd.)
Penguin Group (Australia), 250 Camberwell Road, Camberwell, Victoria 3124, Australia (a division of Pearson Australia Group Pty. Ltd.)
Penguin Books India Pvt. Ltd., 11 Community Centre, Panchsheel Park, New Delhi—110 017, India
Penguin Group (NZ), 67 Apollo Drive, Rosedale, North Shore 0632, New Zealand (a division of Pearson New Zealand Ltd.)
Penguin Books (South Africa) (Pty.) Ltd., 24 Sturdee Avenue, Rosebank, Johannesburg 2196, South Africa

Penguin Books Ltd., Registered Offices: 80 Strand, London WC2R 0RL, England

This book is published in partnership with LucasBooks, a division of Lucasfilm Ltd.

Produced by becker&mayer!, LLC.
11120 NE 33rd Place, Suite 101
Bellevue, WA 98004
www.beckermayer.com

If you have questions or comments about this product, please visit www.beckermayer.com/customerservice.html and click on the Customer Service Request Form.

Written by Pablo Hidalgo
Edited by Delia Greve
Cover designed by Shane Hartley and Mat McInelly
Designed by Mat McInelly
Design assistance by Rosanna Brockley
3-D anaglyph effects by Bill Whitaker, Mat McInelly, and Matthew Fisher
Production management by Larry Weiner

Printed, manufactured, and assembled in China.

ISBN 978-0-448-45583-9 10 9 8 7 6 5 4 3 2 1

09531

Conforms to ASTM standard F9360-08.

My name is Ahsoka Tano and this is my record of some of the important lessons I have learned during my apprenticeship as a Padawan under my Master, Anakin Skywalker. As Jedi serving the Grand Army of the Republic in the Clone Wars, our greatest lessons come from the missions we undertake fighting the Separatists. At the request of the Jedi Council, I am creating a record of those missions so I can pass on what I have learned to future younglings.

Lesson 1:

Have Faith in Your Friends

With missions sending us into the far corners of the galaxy, it's sometimes hard to make time for your true friends. Even though it's difficult, *never* forget them or let them down. They'll be there for you when you most need them.

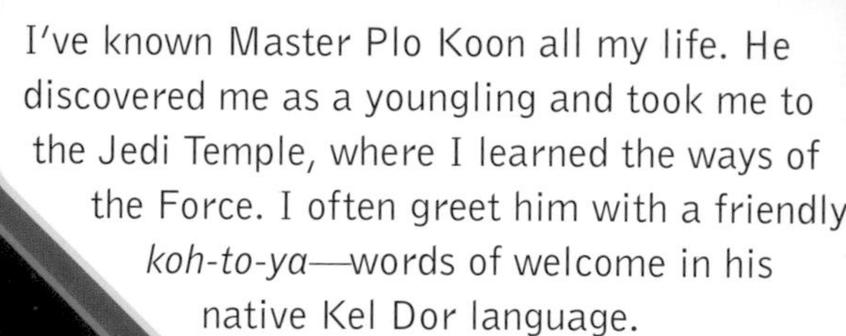

I've known Master Plo Koon all my life. He discovered me as a youngling and took me to the Jedi Temple, where I learned the ways of the Force. I often greet him with a friendly *koh-to-ya*—words of welcome in his native Kel Dor language.

During a clash with the Separatists' mysterious new warship, *Malevolence*, Master Plo's cruiser was torn apart. Plo Koon was the first to get an up-close look at the new warship and its giant ion cannon.

The Jedi Council and the Chancellor had lost all hope that Plo Koon might have survived, but I refused to give up finding him. My Master, Anakin Skywalker, and I used our trusty ship, *Twilight,* to comb the wreckage for all signs of life.

By reaching out with the Force, I sensed Master Plo's presence. He had survived! He hadn't given up hope that someone would come looking for him. Master Plo rallied the clone troopers who had escaped destruction. Even when their air supply ran low and their life pod was surrounded by battle droids, Master Plo *never* gave up.

I wasn't there, but Anakin's chatty protocol droid told me all about the time Viceroy Nute Gunray tried to capture Senator Padmé Amidala. She thought she was paying a diplomatic visit to the people of Rodia. Little did she know, she was walking into a trap!

Nute Gunray had come to Rodia first, and pressured the Rodian Senator to join the Separatists in exchange for supplies they badly needed. So when Senator Amidala arrived, Separatist battle droids surrounded her and took her captive.

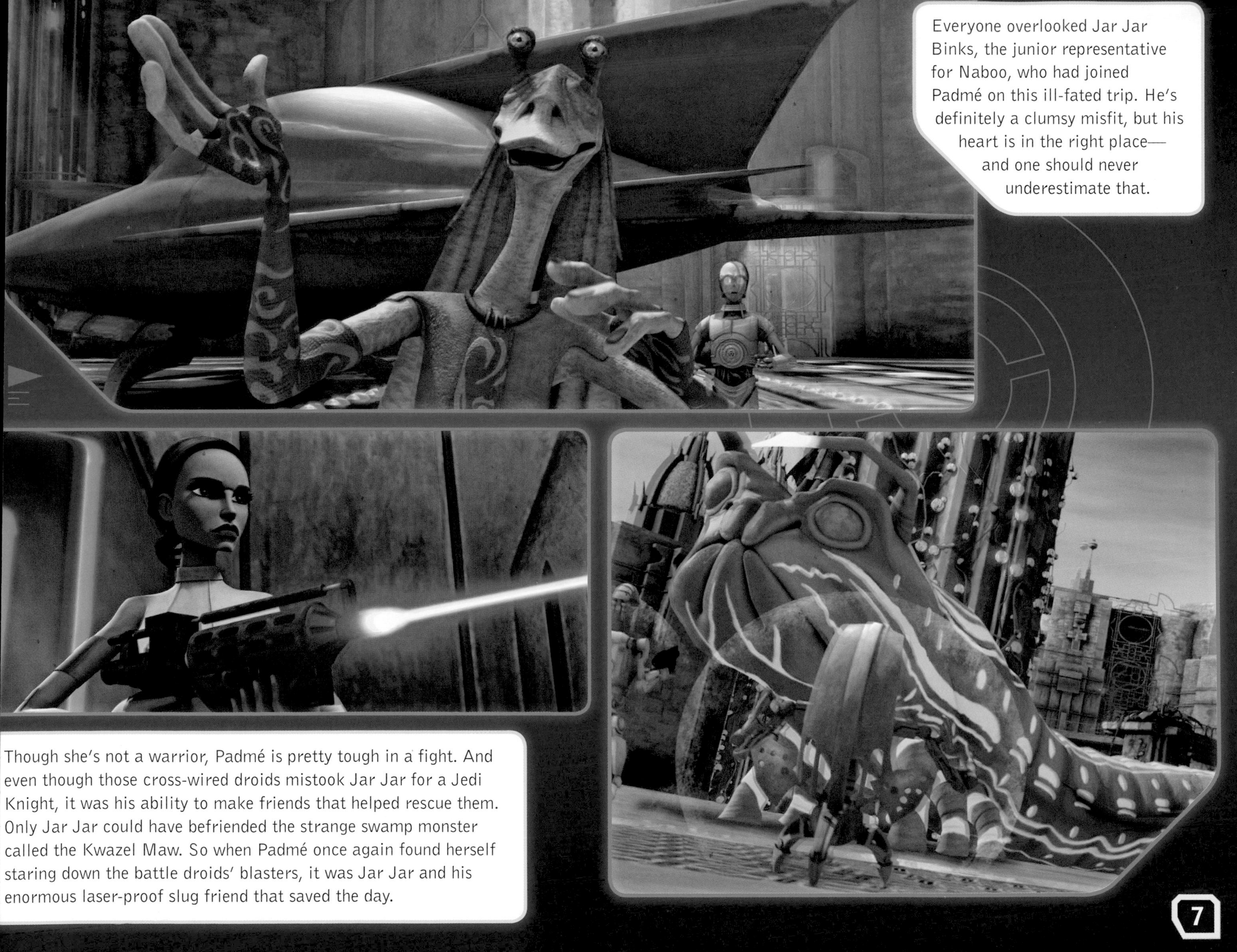
Everyone overlooked Jar Jar Binks, the junior representative for Naboo, who had joined Padmé on this ill-fated trip. He's definitely a clumsy misfit, but his heart is in the right place—and one should never underestimate that.
Though she's not a warrior, Padmé is pretty tough in a fight. And even though those cross-wired droids mistook Jar Jar for a Jedi Knight, it was his ability to make friends that helped rescue them. Only Jar Jar could have befriended the strange swamp monster called the Kwazel Maw. So when Padmé once again found herself staring down the battle droids' blasters, it was Jar Jar and his enormous laser-proof slug friend that saved the day.

The missions to the planet Geonosis were especially difficult. The Clone Wars first started on the harsh, rocky desert planet, and somehow the Separatists had regained control of the enormous droid factories there. We stormed Geonosis with a huge invasion force.

The Geonosian defenses blasted us out of the sky! Our gunships crashed, scattering in the wastelands, and we were separated. But we still had a mission to carry out, and we were determined to reunite and destroy the droid mills. General Ki-Adi-Mundi's forces blazed through the enemy lines with their flamethrower squads.

Anakin and I were together with Captain Rex on our gunship when it crashed near a canyon protected by a thick wall. It was lined with heavy weapons and battle droids. Anakin and I led the attack that brought the wall crashing down—thanks to explosives we slipped into its hollows.

All the members of our invasion team fought past countless Geonosians and battle droids to meet up at our rendezvous point outside the droid factories. We could have all worked separately, but we had faith that the other teams would arrive. United, we destroyed the droid factories.

Lesson 2:

Beware of Traitors!

The enemy is more than just rows of marching battle droids. Those simple tinnies are easy to spot and easy to cut through with a lightsaber. The enemies you *can't* see are more dangerous: Those that hide right in front of you, posing as friends or allies, all the while working against you. You have to keep your eyes open because just one traitor can be more destructive than a thousand battle droids.

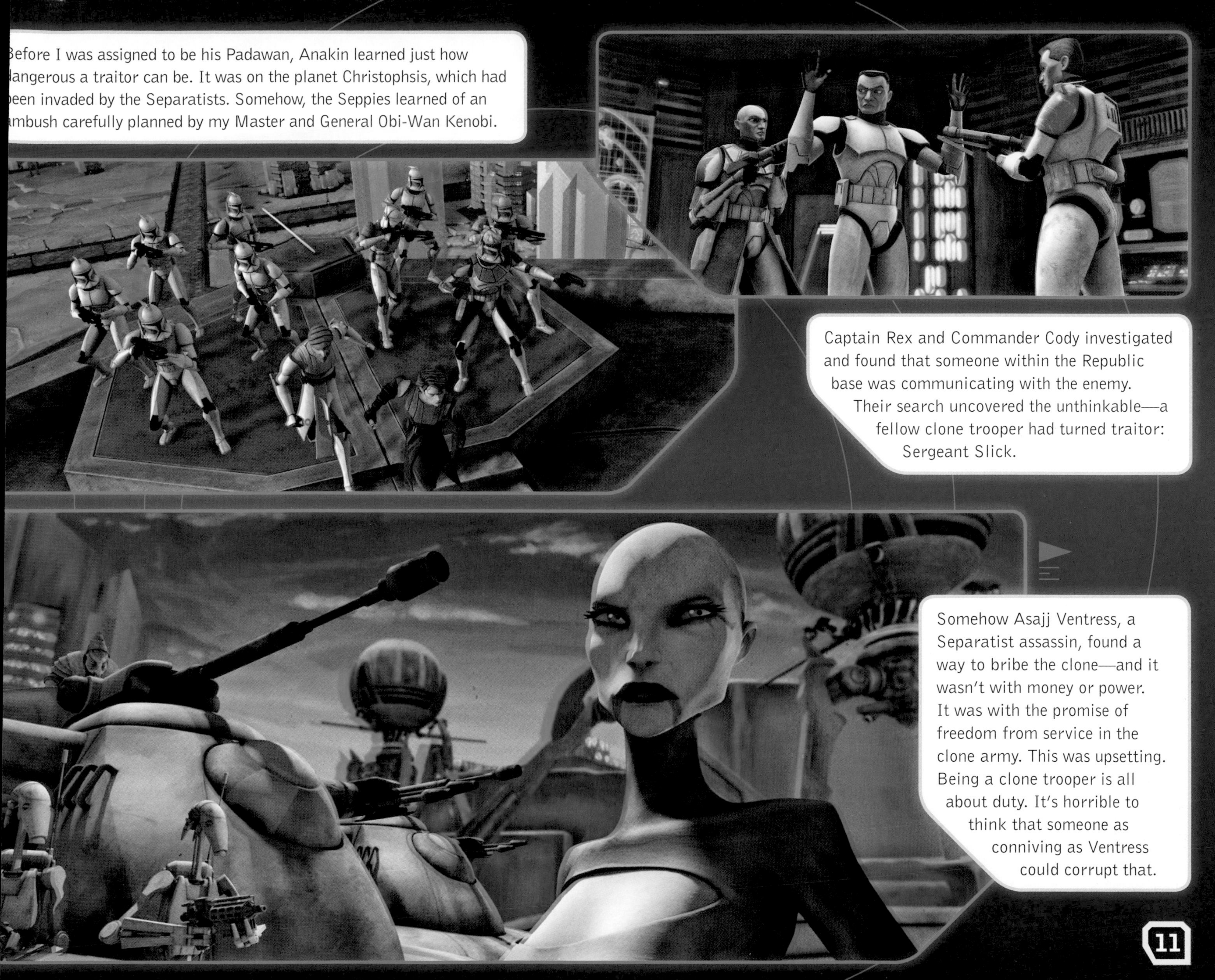
Before I was assigned to be his Padawan, Anakin learned just how dangerous a traitor can be. It was on the planet Christophsis, which had been invaded by the Separatists. Somehow, the Seppies learned of an ambush carefully planned by my Master and General Obi-Wan Kenobi.
Captain Rex and Commander Cody investigated and found that someone within the Republic base was communicating with the enemy. Their search uncovered the unthinkable—a fellow clone trooper had turned traitor: Sergeant Slick.
Somehow Asajj Ventress, a Separatist assassin, found a way to bribe the clone—and it wasn't with money or power. It was with the promise of freedom from service in the clone army. This was upsetting. Being a clone trooper is all about duty. It's horrible to think that someone as conniving as Ventress could corrupt that.

Lesson 2:

Beware of Traitors!

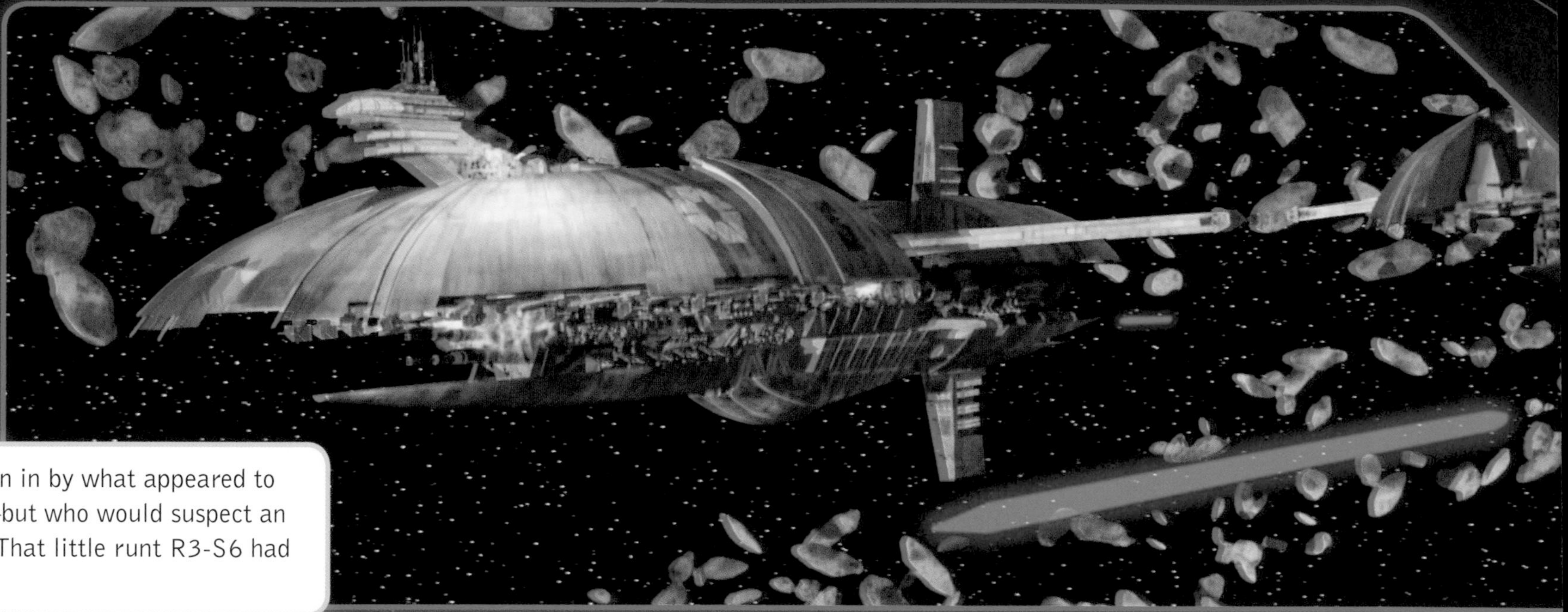

I admit I was taken in by what appeared to be a loyal friend—but who would suspect an astromech droid? That little runt R3-S6 had us all fooled!

It was after the Battle of Bothawui, in a space skirmish where Anakin's starfighter endured heavy damage, that poor R2-D2 disappeared in space debris! We were issued a replacement droid, an advanced R3 unit I nicknamed Goldie. I could tell Anakin was feeling glum about losing Artoo, but I thought he could have been nicer to Goldie. I know Anakin is hard to impress.

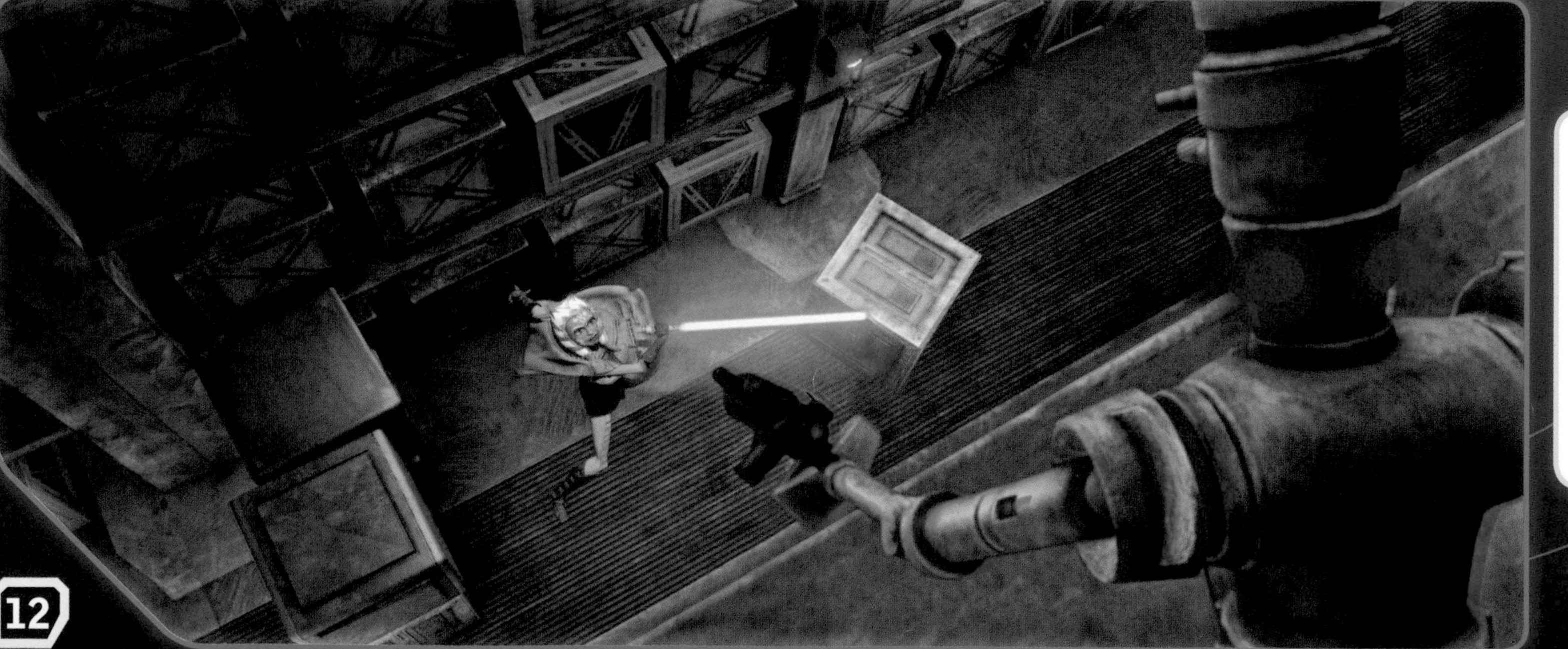

We found a scavenger vessel scouting the asteroids and went aboard to snoop for clues about Artoo. Goldie somehow "accidentally" activated several IG assassin droids that nearly blasted us to bits!

When we tracked an enemy signal to Skytop Station, a Separatist listening outpost, Goldie showed his true colors. The little droid was working for General Grievous, the Separatist leader of the droid army, and nearly trapped us in the station.

We found Artoo captured aboard the station, and thanks to our ever-loyal astromech friend, Goldie's spying days were over.

Lesson 2: **Beware of Traitors!**

One of our costliest losses in th war was because of a traitor who snaked his way deep into our security. It happened after we captured Viceroy Nute Gunray. We held that filthy wealth-worm under heavy guard inside the cruiser *Tranquility*.

I guess Separatist leader Count Dooku didn't want our prisoner spilling secrets because he sent Ventress to capture him. That assassin infiltrated our ship along with some big battle droids by using a boarding craft to break right through our hull. They made a mess of our hangar bay.

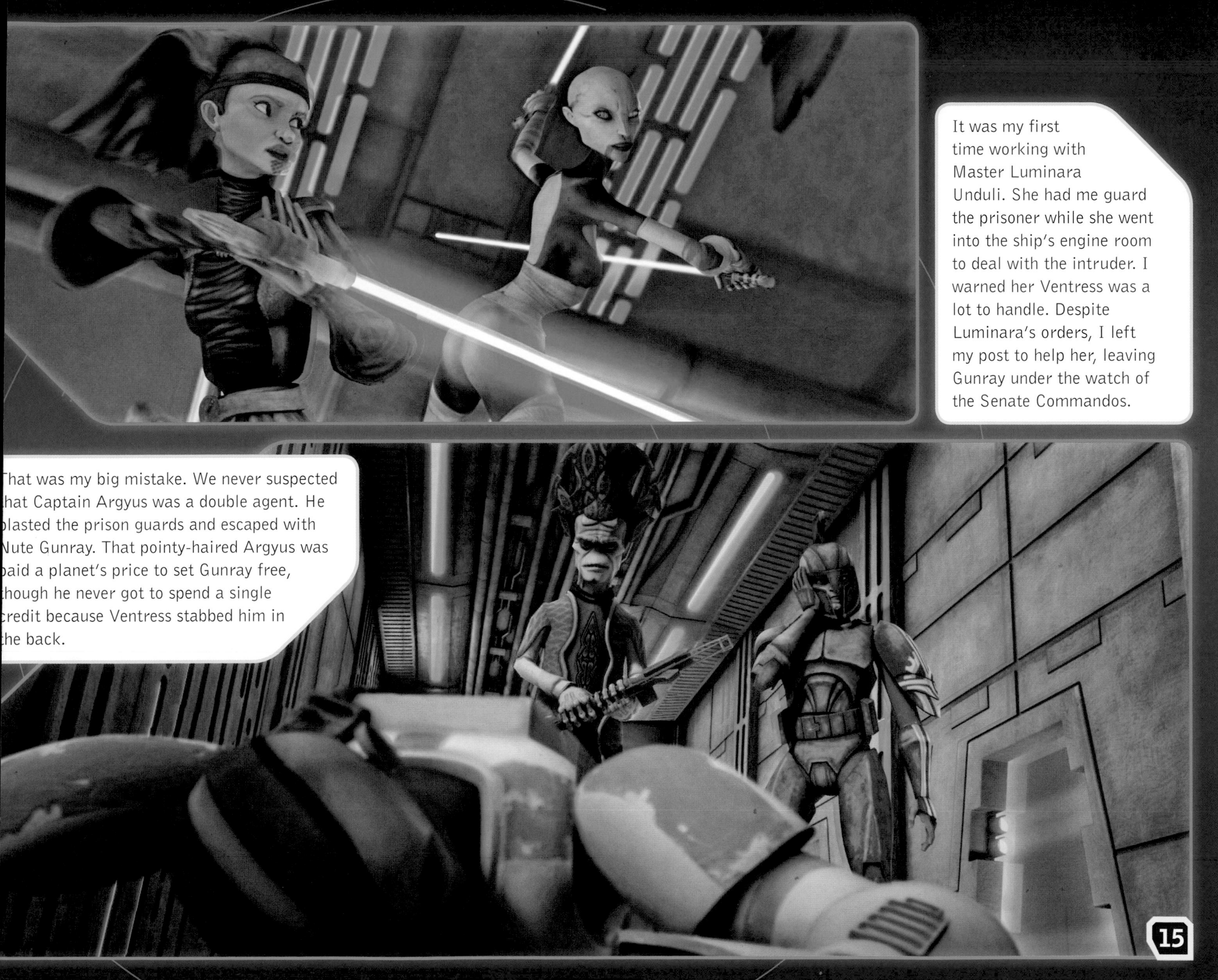
It was my first time working with Master Luminara Unduli. She had me guard the prisoner while she went into the ship's engine room to deal with the intruder. I warned her Ventress was a lot to handle. Despite Luminara's orders, I left my post to help her, leaving Gunray under the watch of the Senate Commandos.
That was my big mistake. We never suspected that Captain Argyus was a double agent. He blasted the prison guards and escaped with Nute Gunray. That pointy-haired Argyus was paid a planet's price to set Gunray free, though he never got to spend a single credit because Ventress stabbed him in the back.

Lesson 2:

Beware of Traitors!

Traitors are hard to spot on the battlefield, but they're even harder to spot in politics. I'd much rather face off against droids and pirates than against Senators and dignitaries—that arena can be much more dangerous than combat because sometimes it's the smiling "ally" who's setting you up for a fall.

My Master, Anakin, told me of his assignment to escort Duchess Satine of Mandalore to the Core World of Coruscant. She was being targeted by a group of Mandalorian rebels, called Death Watch, who didn't like her ideas for preserving peace on her planet.

Somebody snuck deadly assassin probe droids into the hold of the duchess's royal transport. These spindly spiderlike pick-foots stabbed their way through several clone guards until Anakin, along with Captain Rex and Commander Cody, stopped them. Hidden inside each assassin were smaller droids intent on one mission: Kill the duchess!

When the assassin droids couldn't get the job done, they were followed by an invasion of super battle droids. Death Watch rebels were being armed by the Separatists, but it was a double agent who had invited them aboard the royal cruiser to target the duchess. It was her own Senator from Mandalore who tried to kill her. Anakin stopped him in the nick of time, though.

I'll gladly leave the politics to Senator Amidala. She may not have the Force at her side or a lightsaber on her belt, but she can spot a conspiracy brewing or a traitor plotting against the Republic. I read the Coruscant police report when her good friend, Senator Onaconda Farr, was poisoned.

There were plenty of obvious culprits. I think if Anakin or I were on Coruscant at the time, we would have rounded up several of the shiftiest Senators. Even Master Kenobi says politicians aren't to be trusted, though Anakin thinks Chancellor Palpatine is beyond corruption.

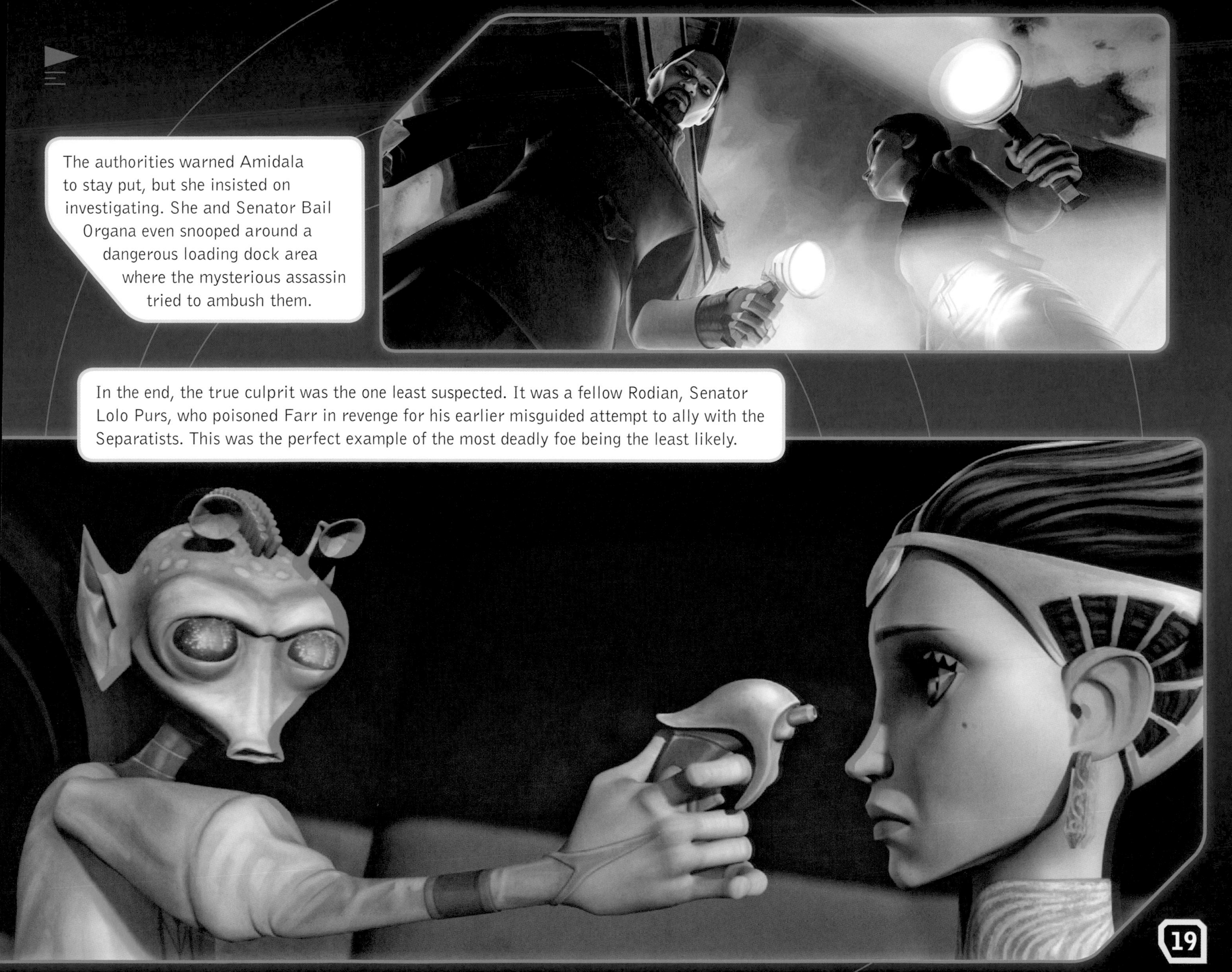

The authorities warned Amidala to stay put, but she insisted on investigating. She and Senator Bail Organa even snooped around a dangerous loading dock area where the mysterious assassin tried to ambush them.

In the end, the true culprit was the one least suspected. It was a fellow Rodian, Senator Lolo Purs, who poisoned Farr in revenge for his earlier misguided attempt to ally with the Separatists. This was the perfect example of the most deadly foe being the least likely.

Lesson 3:

The Galaxy Is Made of People

In this war, when we're huddled around a hologram looking at troop movements and tracking enemy fleets, it's easy to think of the galaxy as just dots on a map. But those dots are the homes of people who have rich histories, pasts, hopes, and fears. We should never forget that.

The people of the planet Toydaria waited cautiously before declaring sides in the war. Because they controlled many resources and trade routes, both the Republic and the Separatists wanted the Toydarians on their side. It was so important for the Republic to sign a treaty with them that Master Yoda himself met with the Toydarian king.

The Separatists aren't ones to play fair, though. They ambushed Yoda when he arrived at the neutral meeting ground. His ship was destroyed, and only Yoda and a trio of clones made it to the surface. Meanwhile, Count Dooku sent Asajj Ventress to persuade the Toydarian king to join the Separatists.

Ventress challenged Yoda and his clone troopers to a contest to impress the oydarians and convince them o join the Separatists. Yoda nd the clones were heavily utnumbered, even though /entress promised a fair ontest. But Yoda inspired the lones to be as resourceful s possible with their limited upplies, and they fought their vay past an entire droid army.

While he could have been forced into joining the Separatists, the Toydarian king instead valued honor and truth. He saw the Separatists as untrustworthy, so he sided with the Republic. It wasn't the strength of firepower that fueled his decision—it was the strength of character.

Even parts of the galaxy that haven't been explored are full of people. After a botched attack damaged our frigate and left Anakin badly injured, we fled into hyperspace. But our ship emerged on a crash course, smashed into the grasslands of an uncharted planet, and we were stranded.

Led by Master Aayla Secura, we found help from the native Lurmen. The small, large-eyed people had natural medicines that stabilized Anakin's weakened condition, and though the people were helpful, I wouldn't call them friendly. Their leader was a strict pacifist, and he didn't want *anything* to do with war.

The Separatists soon arrived, as they so often do to spoil all good, pure things. They planned to use the uncharted planet as a test for their new weapon, a defoliator cannon that destroyed all living matter. It was a horrible device, but the Lurmen still refused to fight, even to defend their world.

Anakin, Aayla, and I fought against the droids and destroyed the defoliator. Although some of the younger Lurmen helped us, their leader held his ground. At first, I wanted to call him a coward, but Master Secura taught me that sticking to your beliefs in the face of death requires a type of courage I had not considered. I may disagree with the Lurmen philosophy, but I respect their right to hold it.

The Jedi were once described as keepers of the peace, not soldiers. The war may forever change that, but studying the mission report about the frozen, uninhabited planet Orto Plutonia gives me hope that the Jedi can still find peaceful resolutions. Master Obi-Wan Kenobi and Anakin went to the planet with dignitaries from its governing moon of Pantora.

Orto Plutonia *was* inhabited, however: A tribe of Talz had been living there for ages. The Pantoran chairman would not abandon his claim to the planet. The Talz wanted only to be left alone, but the chairman found that unacceptable.

The chairman was ready to go to war with the Talz rather than hand Orto Plutonia over to them. The clones were forced to protect the chairman because it was their duty, but Obi-Wan and Anakin did not agree with the chairman's warlike ways. They asked the younger Senator from Pantora to reconsider this violent path.

The chairman thought the primitive natives would be no match for the Pantorans, but a Talz spear proved just as deadly as a blaster bolt. The chairman's dying wish was for the younger Senator to carry on his attack, but she refused. She valued peace more than territory, and respected the Talz. Diplomacy prevailed, and the Pantorans left the planet to its rightful inhabitants.

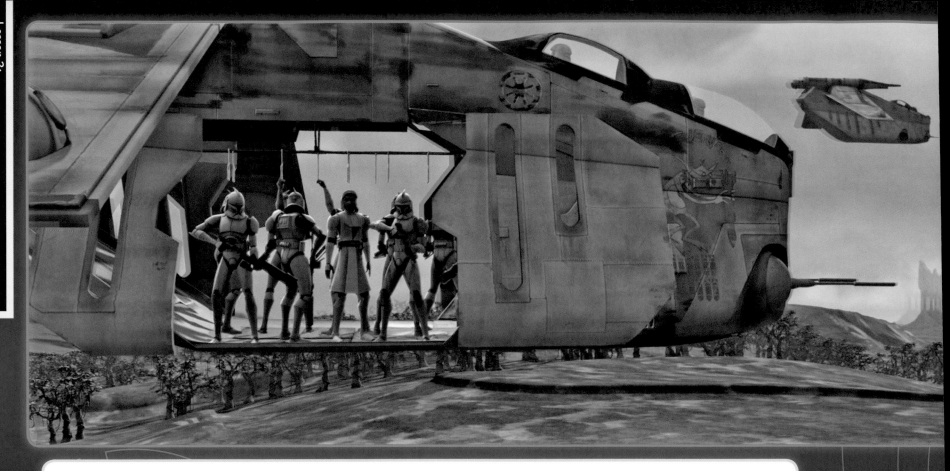

The planet Ryloth is part of the Republic even though it is far from the heart of the galaxy. When the Separatists tried to steal the planet's riches and conquer its people, the Senate sent us to free the native Twi'leks. After Anakin and I broke through the Separatist blockade over the planet, General Obi-Wan's forces cleared a path for the liberation army.

Some of Obi-Wan's soldiers found a young Twi'lek girl living in a bombed village. At first, they probably thought her to be a pest, a little girl who couldn't take care of herself. But believe me—that couldn't be further from the truth!

he girl's name was Numa. Her knowledge of her home helped Obi-Wan's forces ind a series of tunnels that led to the Separatists gunnery outpost. Master Kenobi nd his troops freed the Twi'lek prisoners and destroyed the cannons aimed at our orces.

To retake the capital city, General Windu had help from another local: Cham Syndulla, the leader of the Twi'lek resistance. Many said he was a rebel looking out for only his own power, but General Windu got to know him and saw how much the planet meant to him.

Working with the resistance fighters, General Windu led a heavy assault on the fortress city. He and the Twi'leks cornered the local Separatist leader, and forced him to surrender. We worked together with the Twi'leks to free their world.

Sometimes, people need help to realize the bravery within their hearts. They need to be shown options other than fear. I saw that firsthand on the planet Felucia, when Anakin, Master Obi-Wan, and I were stranded there after a crash landing.

Looking for a way off the planet, we came across a spice-farming village. The villagers lived in constant fear of pillaging pirates. Rather than continue to pay the pirates a portion of their harvest, they hired a quartet of bounty hunters to serve as their protectors.

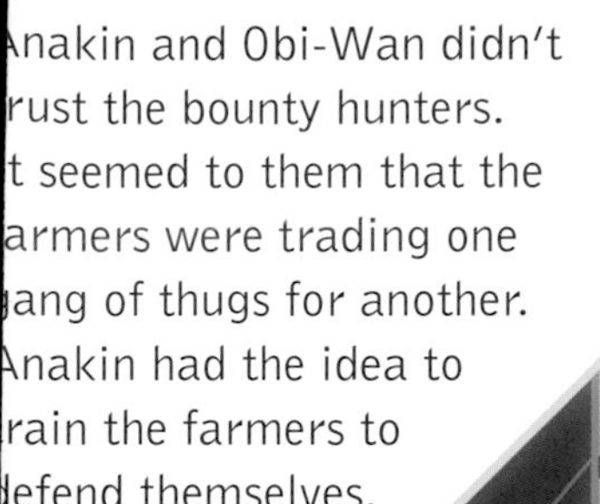

Anakin and Obi-Wan didn't trust the bounty hunters. It seemed to them that the farmers were trading one gang of thugs for another. Anakin had the idea to train the farmers to defend themselves.

In the end when the pirates attacked, the bounty hunters did prove their worth. To their credit, they gave their all to save the villagers. More importantly, though, the villagers organized their own defense, so they could truly be free to determine their own destiny.

The strange forests and wetlands of the planet Saleucami made a perfect hiding place for the Separatist leader of the droid army, General Grievous. Captain Rex led a squad of speeder bike-riding clone troopers to search for that cyborg coward. Commando droids surprised Rex, and badly wounded him with a lucky shot.

His troops rushed Captain Rex to the nearest settlement, a small farm, to heal while they continued their mission. Rex was on his own and his report is strangely incomplete, but he does mention a small family led by a tough farmer named Cut Lawquane.

Bravery can be found anywhere—not just within the Jedi or clone ranks. When commando droids surrounded the farm, Cut fought as fiercely as any clone trooper to protect his family.

I sometimes wonder if even wise Master Yoda can wrap his mind around something as big as a galaxy threatened by war. For me, imagining a family protecting itself from the Separatists makes this war worth fighting.

Lesson 4: Machines Can Be Beaten

The Separatists control many factories across the galaxy that roll out countless droids. If I actually stopped to do the math, it would be a hugely terrifying number, but I'm not afraid—a droid is no equal to a living mind and heart.

The tracking station on the Rishi Moon served as an early warning post for any Separatist attack that might target the cloning centers on the planet Kamino. The rookie clones who worked there thought it was a rather boring assignment, until the day commando droid infiltrators showed up.

These swift and deadly droids did a lot of damage in their first attack, killing the station's commanding officer. That left a team of "shinies"—clones so new their armor was spotless—to fend for themselves.

The droids took over the tracking station, and broadcasted an "all clear" signal to conceal a pending Separatist attack. The clones were greatly outnumbered, but trooper Hevy sacrificed himself to interrupt the signal. The blast that destroyed the station let us know what those Separatists were up to.

Lesson 4: Machines Can Be Beaten

Even the deadliest machines can be brought down by sharp thinking. General Grievous's warship, *Malevolence*, was feared as an unstoppable giant that left no survivors in its path. After surviving our first encounter with it, Anakin, Plo Koon, and I lived to report that it had an ion cannon—a huge weapon that could knock out all the power on a Republic ship, leaving it defenseless.

Anakin didn't focus on what the weapon could do. He instead examined *Malevolence* for weaknesses. Years spent tinkering with machines had taught Anakin there was no weapon that couldn't be broken. It was up to us in Shadow Squadron to break Grievous's new toy.

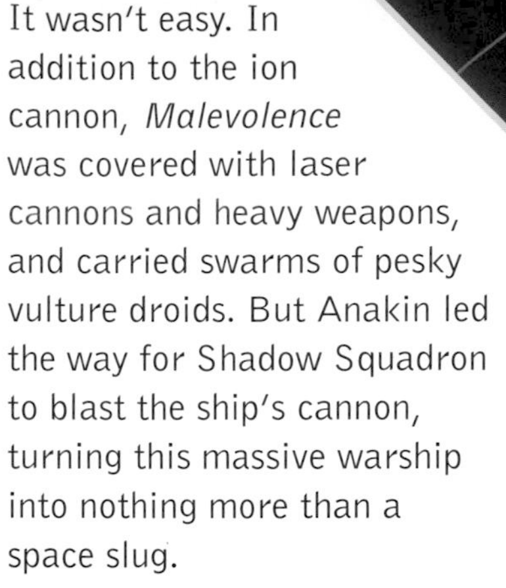

It wasn't easy. In addition to the ion cannon, *Malevolence* was covered with laser cannons and heavy weapons, and carried swarms of pesky vulture droids. But Anakin led the way for Shadow Squadron to blast the ship's cannon, turning this massive warship into nothing more than a space slug.

Anakin and Master Obi-Wan boarded the warship to free Senator Amidala, who was stuck inside as a hostage. Aboard the bridge, Anakin cross-wired the ship's navicomputer so that when *Malevolence* jumped to lightspeed, it would smash into an uninhabited moon.

The bigger the Separatists build 'em, the bigger the explosion will be when my Master and I are through.

During the campaign to retake the planet Geonosis, the Separatists rolled out a new kind of weapon: super tanks with armor so thick, they could deflect just about everything we fired at them. While Anakin and Master Luminara kept the droids busy on the desert surface, Padawan Barriss Offee and I were tasked with destroying the main weapon foundry.

We cut our way through the Geonosian catacombs. It was a creepy maze, but Barriss had memorized every nook and cranny of this nest, and we made our way to the reactor.

However, a few Geonosians caught us planting our explosives, and almost blasted us with a super tank. Barriss was able to take the tank over because the droids driving it weren't very bright.

We lost the explosives, but we had the tank. We used it to blast the reactor. The explosion was tremendous and we should have been turned to dust. But Barriss and I sheltered ourselves from the blast inside the tank. We held out long enough for our Masters to dig us out of the wreckage.

Lesson 5:

This Weapon Is Your Life

A lightsaber is an elegant weapon. More than just a laser sword, the lightsaber is handcrafted by each Jedi. Only through the power of the Force can a Jedi make a lightsaber do some truly amazing things. We must take care of this weapon, the most recognizable symbol of the Jedi Order.

It boils my blood that someone as unworthy as General Grievous carries a lightsaber He didn't earn the right to use one. He's no Knight, but like a spineless scavenger, he takes lightsabers from the bodies of fallen Jedi.

I fought with Grievous aboard Skytop Station. I wasn't afraid of him. Sure, he's bigger, but that just makes him slower and easier to hit. I admit I underestimated him. He may not use the Force, but his cybernetic enhancements make him strong.

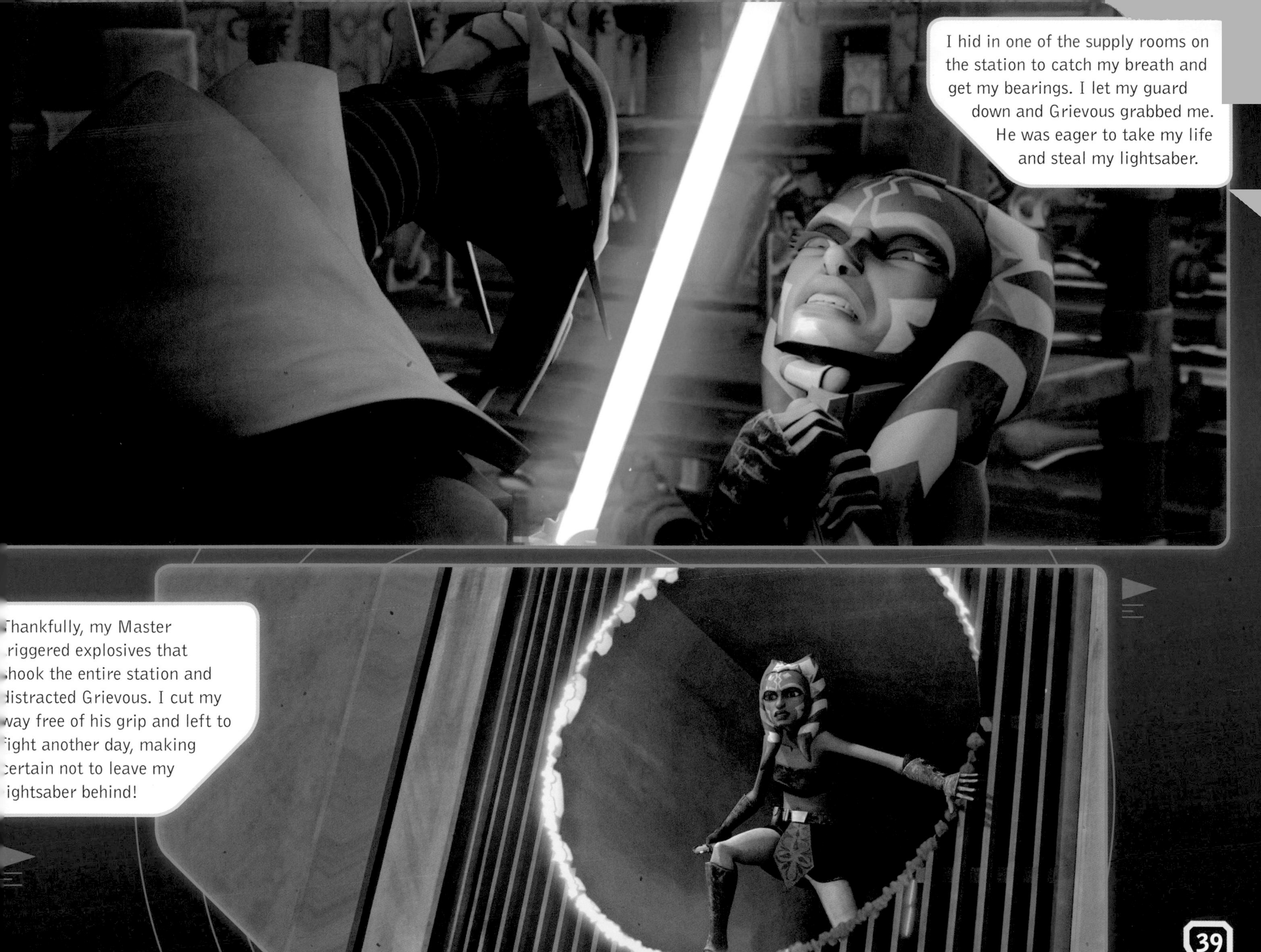
I hid in one of the supply rooms on the station to catch my breath and get my bearings. I let my guard down and Grievous grabbed me. He was eager to take my life and steal my lightsaber.
Thankfully, my Master riggered explosives that hook the entire station and listracted Grievous. I cut my vay free of his grip and left to ight another day, making ertain not to leave my ightsaber behind!

Somewhere deep within a secret lair hidden in the crags of the moon Vassek, General Grievous keeps a trophy room to celebrate his victories against the Jedi. This grim trove is filled with stolen lightsabers, severed Padawan braids, and statues that honor his feats as a warrior.

Jedi Master Kit Fisto and his former Padawan Nahdar Vebb found this lair when on a mission to track an escaped Separatist prisoner. Grievous was not happy about them intruding, but he relished the chance to add to his collection.

Poor Nahdar. He attacked Grievous, thinking he could take the general all on his own. He let his anger cloud his judgment, and he underestimated Grievous, who blasted Nahdar in the back during a lightsaber duel. Grievous then began using Nahdar's lightsaber as his own.

Master Fisto dueled Grievous, who didn't waste time turning it into an unfair fight by bringing in his bodyguard droids. Kit Fisto reclaimed Nahdar's lightsaber by cutting off one of Grievous's mechanical limbs, and then escaped, making sure the weapon never ended up in Grievous's trophy room.

This is so embarrassing, but perhaps the lessons that stick with you the most are those you learn from your own mistakes. While Anakin and I were zeroing in on a weapons dealer in the slums of Coruscant, a pickpocket stole my lightsaber!

Jedi Master Tera Sinube helped me identify the culprit, and we returned to the underworld to find the fishy thief.

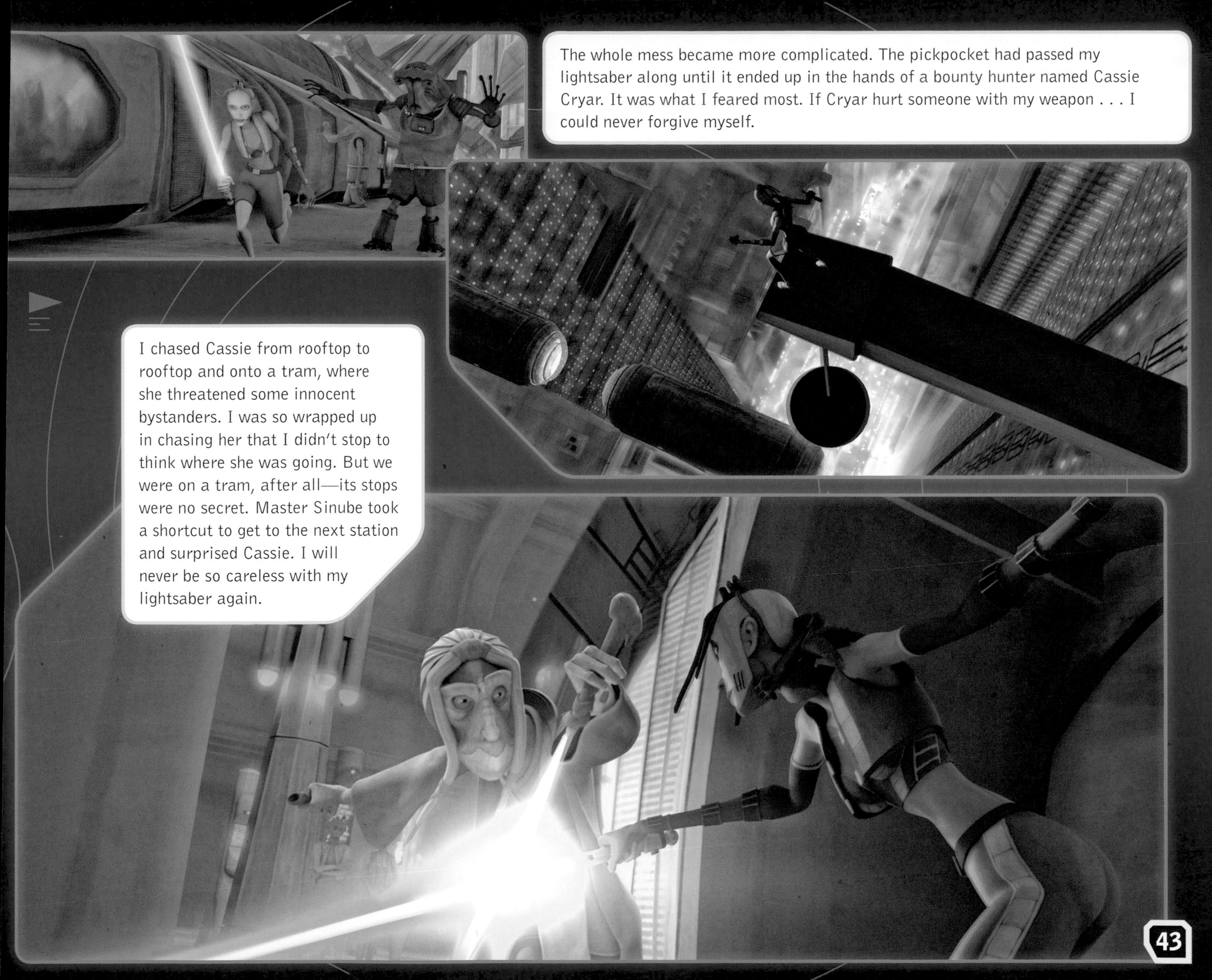
The whole mess became more complicated. The pickpocket had passed my lightsaber along until it ended up in the hands of a bounty hunter named Cassie Cryar. It was what I feared most. If Cryar hurt someone with my weapon . . . I could never forgive myself.
I chased Cassie from rooftop to rooftop and onto a tram, where she threatened some innocent bystanders. I was so wrapped up in chasing her that I didn't stop to think where she was going. But we were on a tram, after all—its stops were no secret. Master Sinube took a shortcut to get to the next station and surprised Cassie. I will never be so careless with my lightsaber again.

Lesson 6:

Know Your Enemy

Study every scrap of information you can about your enemy. They're often creatures of habit with patterns you can predict. As slippery as some of these lowlifes are, they can often be defeated by their own oversights.

General Grievous captured Jedi Master Eeth Koth in a raid, and he couldn't help but gloat about it to the Jedi Council via hologram. Master Koth took advantage of Grievous's vanity, and used secret hand signals while in the hologram to let us know where he was being held prisoner.

This led to a big space battle. As Master Obi-Wan Kenobi led the fleet to engage Grievous's destroyer, Anakin and Master Adi Gallia snuck aboard Grievous's ship and the general went aboard Obi-Wan's cruiser to fight.

/e were *both* trying to outsmart the
ther! While we lured Grievous off
is warship, Grievous lured Anakin
nd Adi Gallia into a trap. Just as
ny Master was about to free
eth Koth, he was surrounded
y commando droids.

As much as we underestimated Grievous, he misjudged the Jedi as well. Grievous got away, but he escaped empty-handed. Anakin rescued Master Koth, and we kept Grievous's warship. He'll think twice before trying to lure us into a trap again.

According to ancient texts, the people of Mandalore have a history marked by war and violence. But they are isolated and have filled the galaxy with misconceptions about them.

The idea of a Mandalorian pacifist came as a surprise when Duchess Satine of Mandalore became the head of the Council of Neutral Systems—a group of 1,500 worlds that refused to take sides in the Clone Wars. Some believed it to be a lie, and that she was secretly building an army for Count Dooku.

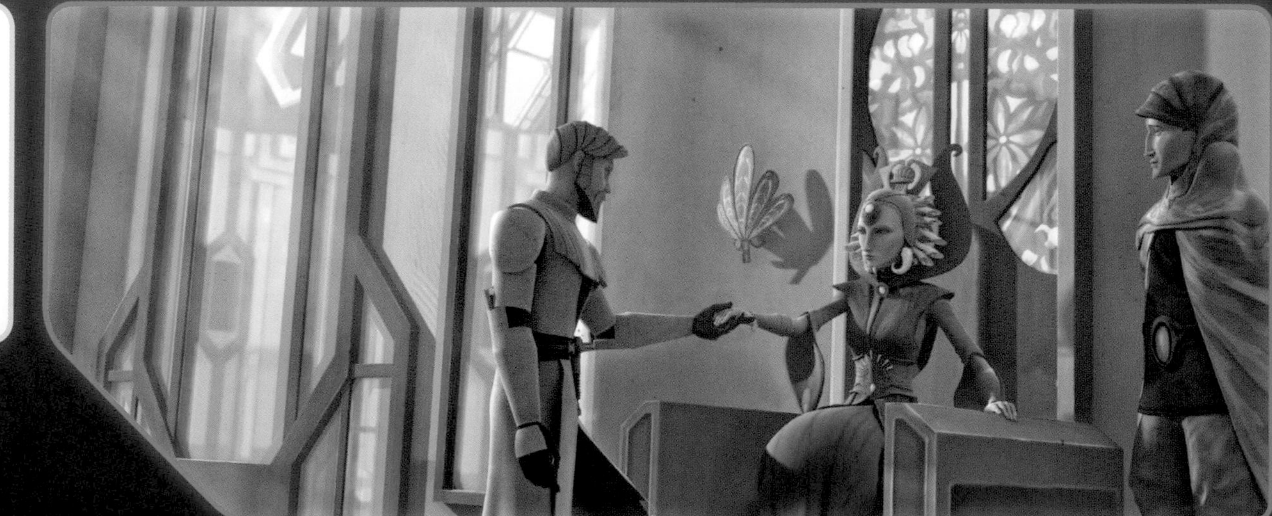

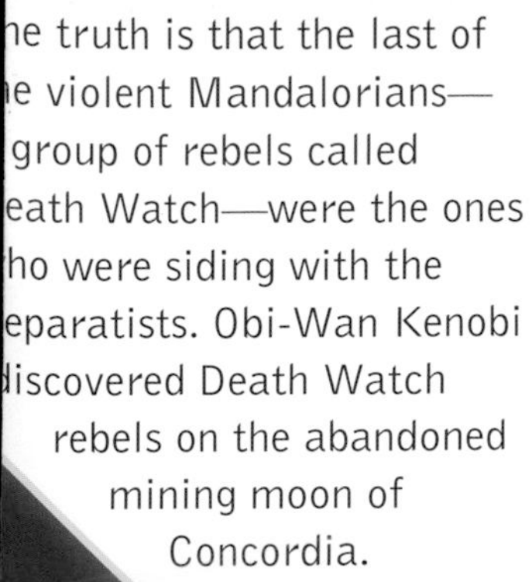

he truth is that the last of he violent Mandalorians— group of rebels called eath Watch—were the ones ho were siding with the eparatists. Obi-Wan Kenobi iscovered Death Watch rebels on the abandoned mining moon of Concordia.

Someone else knew this, too. Someone created evidence to show that Death Watch was active on the planet in an attempt to push the Republic into occupying Mandalore. If that had happened, we would have been seen as invaders, and Death Watch rebels would have been seen as heroes! But the duchess knew her people better than we did. She stayed true to her convictions and uncovered the plot!

The Republic was prepared to fortify Mandalore and protect it against Death Watch. But the duchess didn't want our help. She was afraid her people would see the Republic as an invader.

Before I was apprenticed to Anakin, he was working with Admiral Yularen during the Battle of Christophsis. The crystal world was blockaded by the Separatists, under the command of Admiral Trench.

Yularen had encountered Trench before and understood what kind of enemy the Republic faced. He knew Trench could not be taken lightly. Anakin agreed and decided he had to do something about Trench, even though it wasn't his primary mission.

nakin and Yularen were ssigned to fly a stealth ship ast the blockade and deliver upplies to the surface. Instead, my Master took the fight to Trench. Based n Yularen's experience and a quick look t Trench's war record, Anakin knew the eparatist admiral couldn't resist firing oming torpedoes at the stealth ship.

Only Anakin could have pulled off flying hull-to-hull with Trench's ship, dragging the torpedoes right back at the enemy. But it was the knowledge Yularen and Anakin had of their enemy that helped them bring down Trench's warship, and open the blockade.

Lesson 7:

Respect the Natural World

With our lightsaber blades, we Jedi can deflect laser bolts. Our clone troopers wear hardened armor to protect themselves from the enemy. But there are some threats that aren't so easily guarded against. When the war spills over into the wilderness, we need to be especially careful because nature often bites back.

Leave it to the Separatists to corrupt nature into a weapon. The insane Doctor Nuvo Vindi took a long-extinct virus and changed it into a deadly airborne strain. He tested it on the planet Naboo, which could have led to a disastrous outbreak.

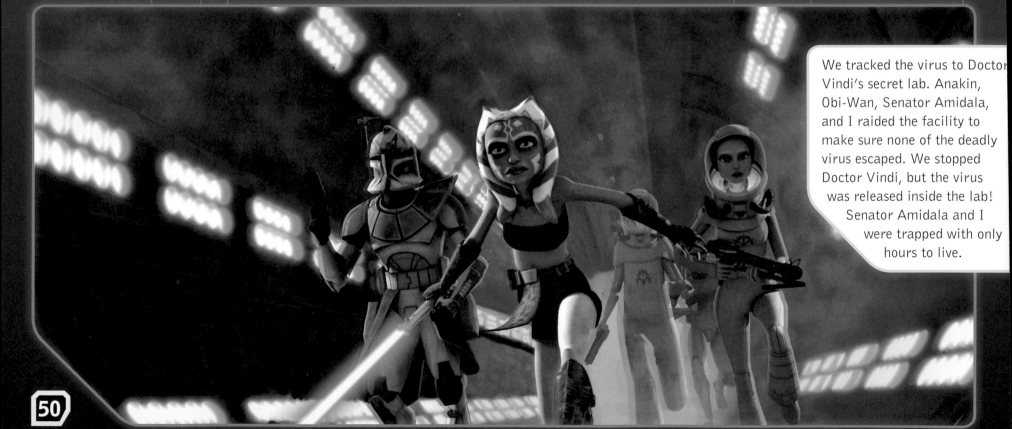

We tracked the virus to Doctor Vindi's secret lab. Anakin, Obi-Wan, Senator Amidala, and I raided the facility to make sure none of the deadly virus escaped. We stopped Doctor Vindi, but the virus was released inside the lab! Senator Amidala and I were trapped with only hours to live.

My Master and Obi-Wan found a potential cure in the reeksa root, a plant located only on Iego, the world of a thousand moons. They had to crawl into deep crevices and fend off angry snapping plants to cut a sample of the root.

Escaping Iego was not easy, either. The Separatists had lined he moons with a powerful aser-trap. My Master was ble to weave *Twilight* hrough that deadly mesh f light and return to aboo with the cure.

It was a close call. I nearly paid the price for the Separatists' tampering with nature, but we cured the virus before it could spread.

Life-forms have an astounding variety of shapes and behaviors. We thought we knew enough about the Geonosians to reconquer their planet. But they had a few natural surprises in store for us.

There had long been a rumor about a Geonosian queen who was said to control the mind of her hive, but there were no details about how she did it. When our mission to Geonosis took us deep under the planet's surface, we began to uncover some of the unsettling details.

he Geonosian queen used brain worms to influence her hive. A squirmy worm would wriggle its way through the mouth or nostril of its victim and wrap itself around the brain stem. The worm's hold was so powerful, it could even animate the dead! I shudder thinking about Geonosian zombies.

Some of these worms invaded a Republic medical frigate that Barriss and I were aboard. Our clone troopers turned on us because the worms were controlling them. Even Barriss got infected, leaving me alone to defend the ship.

Fortunately, our research revealed that the worms could not stand extreme cold. I ruptured the frigate's coolant system and plunged the ship into a deep freeze. That way, I could save the clones and Barriss, and stop the worms from getting any farther.

When the Separatists nearly overran the planet Malastare—an important planet because of its deep fuel reserves—the Republic was forced to do something desperate. We dropped a massive electro-proton bomb on the enemy, which shorted out all their battle droids. But it also woke up something huge and cranky from a long slumber.

The people of Malastare called the creature the Zillo Beast, and the monster was the last of its kind. The people refused to sign a treaty with the Republic unless we agreed to destroy the beast, but to kill an innocent life-form is against the way of the Jedi. Chancellor Palpatine insisted we agree to destroy it, so the Republic could have fuel to continue the war.

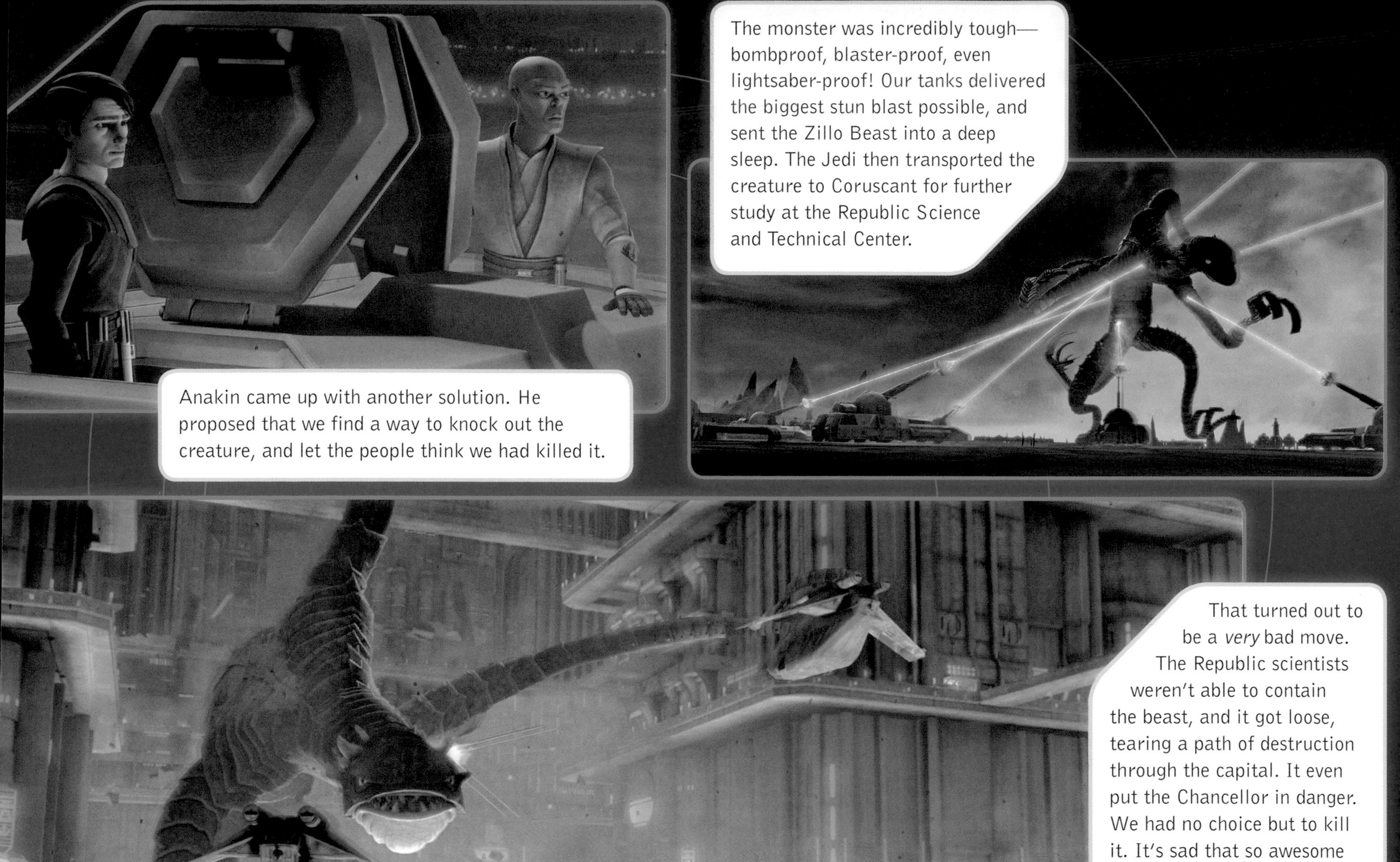

The monster was incredibly tough—bombproof, blaster-proof, even lightsaber-proof! Our tanks delivered the biggest stun blast possible, and sent the Zillo Beast into a deep sleep. The Jedi then transported the creature to Coruscant for further study at the Republic Science and Technical Center.

Anakin came up with another solution. He proposed that we find a way to knock out the creature, and let the people think we had killed it.

That turned out to be a *very* bad move. The Republic scientists weren't able to contain the beast, and it got loose, tearing a path of destruction through the capital. It even put the Chancellor in danger. We had no choice but to kill it. It's sad that so awesome a creature paid for our mistakes with its life.

Lesson 8:

Keep Your Eyes on Scoundrels

There are more dangers lurking in the galaxy than mindless droids or ambitious Separatist generals. There are neutral forces that want to turn the war into a tidy profit by playing by their own rules. Of all these scoundrels lurking on the fringe, pirates and bounty hunters are the craftiest.

The fringe doesn't exist in any one place in the galaxy—even the heart of the Republic, Coruscant, isn't safe from lowlifes like bounty hunters. Cad Bane and a posse of predators attacked the Galactic Senate building. That took nerves of carbonite to pull off!

Cad Bane held a group of Senators hostage and made his demands of the Chancellor directly. The whole thing was a prison break. Bane wanted to free Ziro the Hutt from jail.

My Master was caught in the Senate building during the hostage crisis. He was unarmed at the time (Master, whatever happened to "This weapon is your life"?), so he had to improvise a way of getting past the hunters.

Thanks to Senator Amidala, Anakin was able to free the hostages—but the bounty hunters got away with their prize.

When Cad Bane broke into the Jedi Temple, he went so far as to have his partner, a shape-shifter, pose as the librarian, Jocasta Nu. I saw through her disguise and caught this bounty hunter in the act.

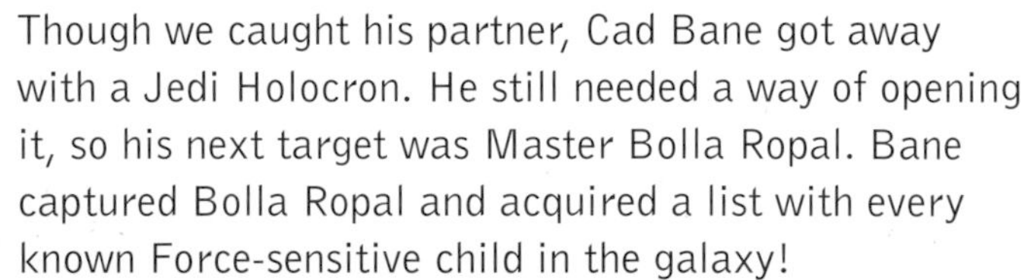

Though we caught his partner, Cad Bane got away with a Jedi Holocron. He still needed a way of opening it, so his next target was Master Bolla Ropal. Bane captured Bolla Ropal and acquired a list with every known Force-sensitive child in the galaxy!

Cad Bane moved on from thief to kidnapper. He began targeting potential younglings for his evil plot. I stopped him in time on Naboo, and we finally captured the bounty hunter. But we couldn't hold him for long.

We never discovered who was the mastermind behind Bane's plot, but we did find the other kidnapped children on the fiery world of Mustafar. Anakin and I were able to save the babies before the whole Mustafar base came crashing down into the lava.

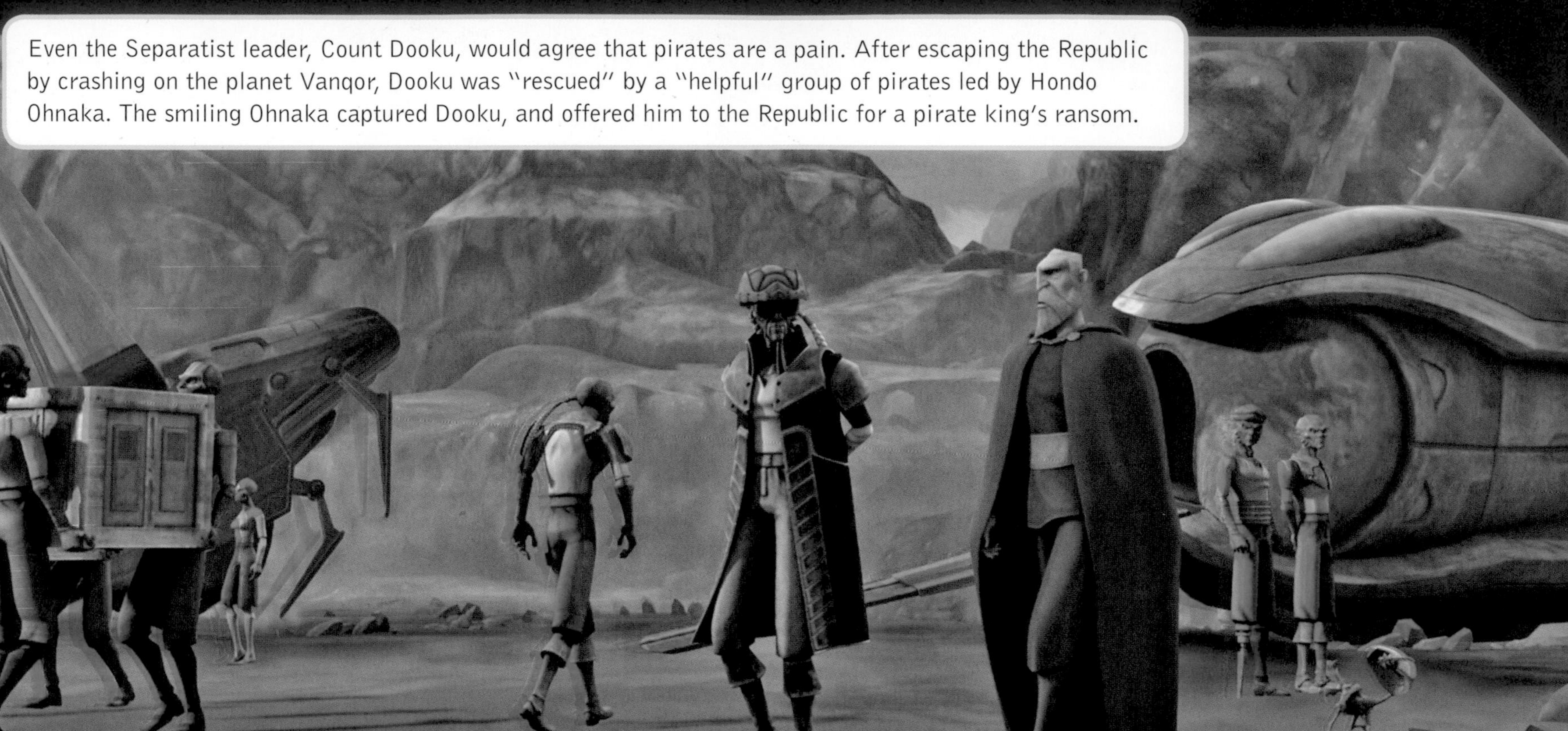

Even the Separatist leader, Count Dooku, would agree that pirates are a pain. After escaping the Republic by crashing on the planet Vanqor, Dooku was "rescued" by a "helpful" group of pirates led by Hondo Ohnaka. The smiling Ohnaka captured Dooku, and offered him to the Republic for a pirate king's ransom.

Master Obi-Wan and Anakin voyaged to the pirate's den on the planet Florrum to make sure Dooku was their prisoner. But Ohnaka's greed outweighed his common sense. He drugged Obi-Wan and Anakin, thinking he could get triple the ransom with two more Jedi prisoners.

Holding a Jedi isn't easy. While the Republic gathered the ransom for delivery, Obi-Wan and Anakin managed to escape—still shackled to Dooku! If there is anything in the galaxy that could get the Jedi to work *with* Dooku, it's pirates.

During the escape, Count Dooku split from the Jedi and would go on to cause more trouble. But here's where Obi-Wan stood light years apart from a pirate like Ohnaka. Master Obi-Wan walked away from the pirate den without making Ohnaka pay for his treachery. The pirates no longer had Dooku, so they had nothing at all that interested the Jedi.

Bounty hunters are rotten to the core, that's for sure. Young Boba Fett could have lived a life different than the one of his father, Jango Fett. But he was taken under the wing of that villain, Aurra Sing. She helped sneak Boba aboard the Jedi cruiser *Endurance* where he blended in perfectly with a group of young clones.

Boba wanted revenge against Mace Windu, the Jedi who had killed his father, so he snuck a powerful explosive into Mace's quarters. Master Windu narrowly avoided being blasted into cinders. Boba then sent the whole cruiser crashing onto the planet Vanqor by sabotaging its main reactor.

When Master Windu and Anakin searched the wreckage for survivors, they found a trap waiting for them. With the help of fellow bounty hunters, Boba rigged an explosive souvenir for Mace Windu: His father's helmet packed with a bomb. Anakin and Master Windu were lucky to escape alive, but they were both badly injured.

oba didn't give up.
e tried to lure the
edi Master once
ore. The bounty
unters took hostages
nd, in a transmission
ent to the Jedi
emple, said they'd
ill the prisoners if
laster Windu didn't
how up.

But Mace was in no condition to travel, so Master Plo and I scoured for clues in the Coruscant underworld. That's where we found a tip that Aurra Sing was spotted on the planet Florrum. We traveled to the bounty hunter's hideout to bring Boba to justice.

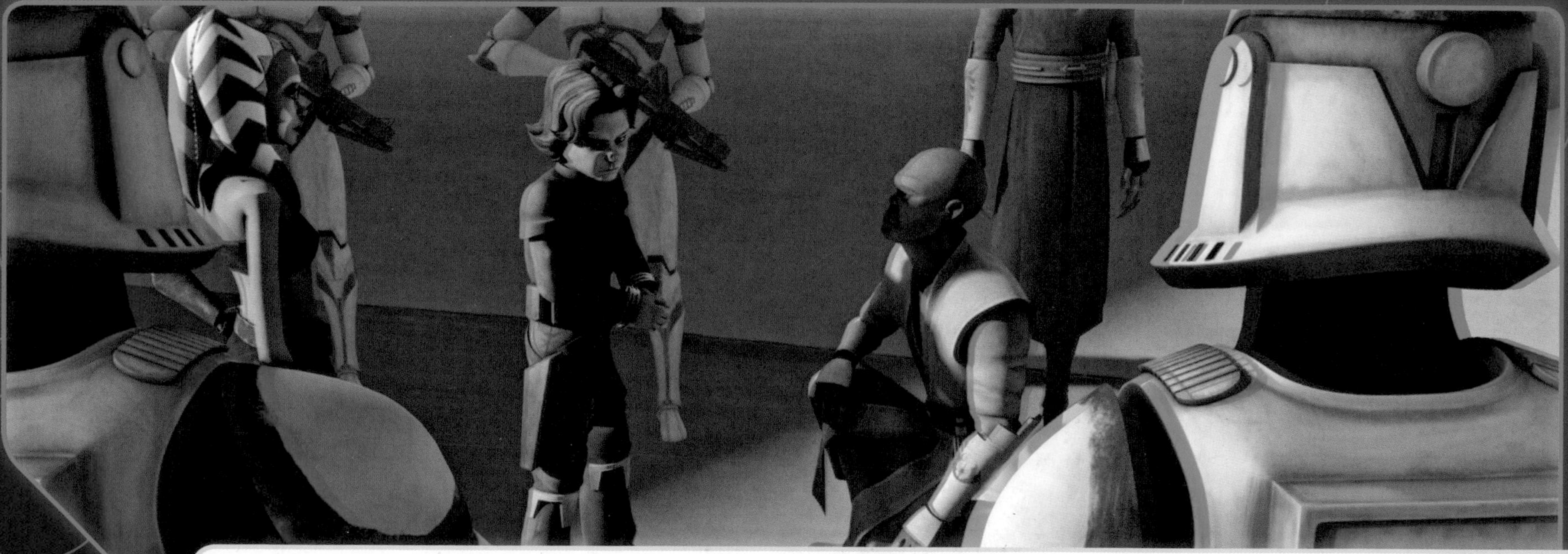

Justice. That's what Boba said he wanted. He said he didn't want to hurt any innocents in his hunt, but I don't know if I can trust what a bounty hunter says—especially one raised by Aurra Sing. When Master Plo and I arrived, Aurra abandoned Boba. He's in custody now. Only the Force knows what the future holds for him . . . but I'm sure there are a few more lessons for us all to learn.